Based on the TV series *Blue's Clues*® created by Traci Paige Johnson,
Todd Kessler, and Angela C. Santomero as seen on Nick Jr.®
On *Blue's Clues*, Joe is played by Donovan Patton.
Photos by Joan Marcus.

SIMON SPOTLIGHT
An imprint of Simon & Schuster Children's Publishing Division
1230 Avenue of the Americas, New York, New York 10020
Manufactured in the United States of America
First Edition
2 4 6 8 10 9 7 5 3 1
ISBN 0-689-84971-0

Blue's 12 Days of Christmas

by Catherine Lukas
illustrated by Karen Craig

Simon Spotlight/Nick Jr.
New York   London   Toronto   Sydney   Singapore

On the first day of Christmas
my good friend gave to me:

a star for the top of our tree!

On the second day of Christmas
my good friends gave to me:

two purple doves

and a star for the top of our tree!

On the third day of Christmas
my good friends gave to me:

three tin men,

two purple doves,
and a star for the top of our tree!

On the fourth day of Christmas
my good friends gave to me:

four paper chains,

three tin men,
two purple doves,
and a star for the top of our tree!

On the fifth day of Christmas
my good friends gave to me:

five popcorn strings . . .

four paper chains,
three tin men,
two purple doves,
and a star
for the top of our tree!

On the sixth day of Christmas
my good friends gave to me:

six bells for sleighing,

five popcorn strings . . .
four paper chains,
three tin men,
two purple doves,
and a star for the top of our tree!

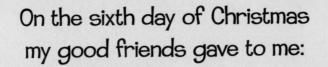

On the seventh day of Christmas
my good friends gave to me:

seven songs for singing,

six bells for sleighing,
five popcorn strings . . .
four paper chains,
three tin men,
two purple doves,
and a star for the top of our tree!

On the eighth day of Christmas
my good friends gave to me:

eight balls a-clinking,

seven songs for singing,
six bells for sleighing,
five popcorn strings . . .
four paper chains,
three tin men,
two purple doves,
and a star for the top of our tree!

On the ninth day of Christmas
my good friends gave to me:

nine cards for mailing,

eight balls a-clinking,
seven songs for singing,
six bells for sleighing,
five popcorn strings . . .
four paper chains,
three tin men,
two purple doves,
and a star for the top of our tree!

On the tenth day of Christmas
my good friends gave to me:

ten lights a-blinking,

nine cards for mailing,
eight balls a-clinking,
seven songs for singing,
six bells for sleighing,
five popcorn strings . . .
four paper chains,
three tin men,
two purple doves,
and a star for the top of our tree!

tree
lights

On the eleventh day of Christmas
my good friends gave to me:

eleven cookies cooling,

ten lights a-blinking,
nine cards for mailing,
eight balls a-clinking,
seven songs for singing,
six bells for sleighing,
five popcorn strings . . .
four paper chains,
three tin men,
two purple doves,
and a star for the top of our tree!

On the twelfth day of Christmas
my good friends gave to me:

twelve stockings hanging,

eleven cookies cooling,
ten lights a-blinking,
nine cards for mailing,
eight balls a-clinking,
seven songs for singing,
six bells for sleighing,
five popcorn strings . . .
four paper chains,
three tin men,
two purple doves,
and a star for the top of our tree!